Let's Count the Raindrops

illustrations by

Fumi Kosaka

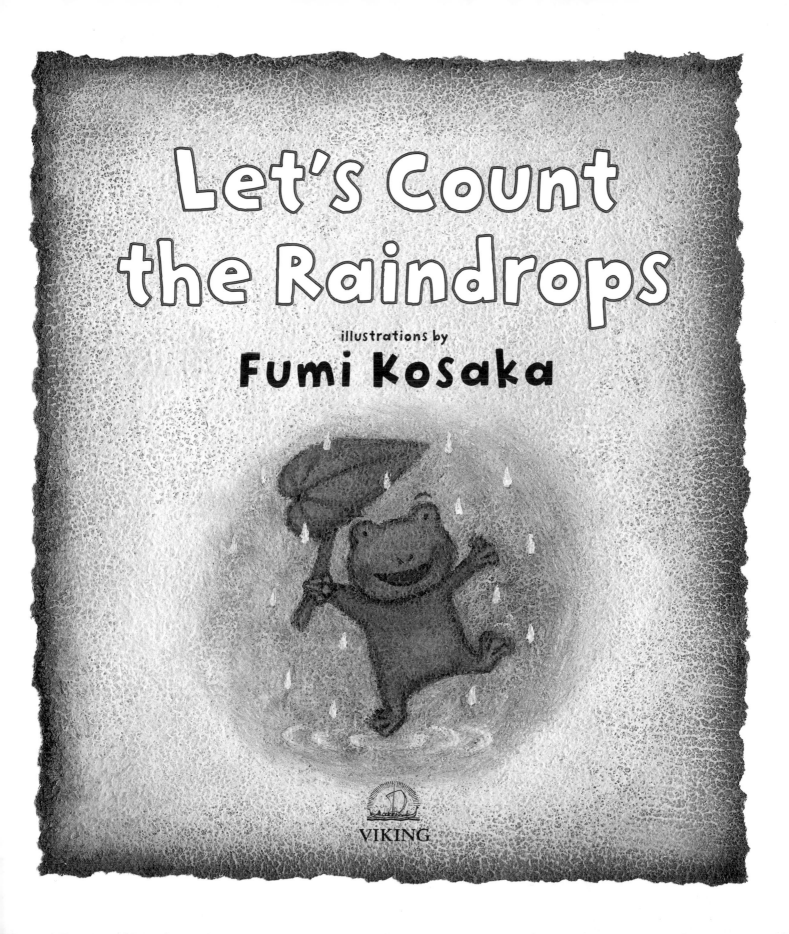

VIKING

Weather

Whether the weather be fine
Or whether the weather be not,
Whether the weather be cold
Or whether the weather be hot,
We'll weather the weather
Whatever the weather,
Whether we like it or not.

Anonymous

The Sun

I told the Sun that I was glad,
   I'm sure I don't know why;
Somehow the pleasant way he had
   of shining in the sky,
Just put a notion in my head
   That wouldn't it be fun
If, walking on the hill, I said
   "I'm happy" to the Sun.

John Drinkwater

June!

The day is warm
and a breeze is blowing,
the sky is blue
and its eye is glowing,
and everything's new
and green and growing. . . .

My shoes are off
and my socks are showing. . . .

My socks are off. . . .

Do you know how I'm going?

BAREFOOT!

Aileen Fisher

Wouldn't You?

If I
Could go
As high
And low
As the wind
As the wind
As the wind
Can blow—

I'd go!

John Ciardi

Clouds

White sheep, white sheep,
On a blue hill,
When the wind stops
You all stand still
When the wind blows
You walk away slow.
White sheep, white sheep,
Where do you go?

Christina G. Rossetti

Let's Count
the Raindrops

Let's count the raindrops
as they pour:
one million, two million,
three million, four.

Alan Benjamin

The Leaves Fall Down

One by one the leaves fall down
From the sky come falling one by one
And leaf by leaf the summer is done
One by one by one by one.

Margaret Wise Brown

Fog and clouds are not allowed
to spoil my sunny day.

I want to shout and run about
and go outside and play.

Peggy Guthart

The Silent Snow

The snow is so quiet,
the snow is so white,
TONS of it fell
from the sky last night;
It came in a hurry
without any warning—
I WAS so surprised when
I woke up this morning.

Ivy O. Eastwick

Winter Clothes

Under my hood I have a hat
And under that
My hair is flat.
Under my coat
My sweater's blue.
My sweater's red.
I'm wearing two.
My muffler muffles to my chin
And round my neck
And then tucks in.

My gloves were knitted
By my aunts.
I've mittens too
And pants
And pants
And boots
And shoes
With socks inside.
The boots are rubber, red and wide.
And when I walk
I must not fall
Because I can't get up at all.

Karla Kuskin

To my wonderful parents!

VIKING

Published by the Penguin Group

Penguin Putnam Books for Young Readers, 345 Hudson Street, New York, New York 10014, U.S.A.

Penguin Books Ltd, Registered Offices: Harmondsworth, Middlesex, England

First published in 2001 by Viking, a division of Penguin Putnam Books for Young Readers.

1 3 5 7 9 10 8 6 4 2

LIBRARY OF CONGRESS CATALOGING-IN-PUBLICATION DATA

Let's count the raindrops / illustrated by Fumi Kosaka.

p.   cm.

ISBN 0-670-89689-6

1. Weather—Juvenile poetry.   2. Children's poetry, American.   3. Children's poetry, English.

[1. Weather—Poetry.   2. American poetry—Collections.   3. English poetry—Collections.]   I. Kosaka, Fumi, ill.

PS595.W38 L48 2001   811.008'036—dc21   00–010683

Printed in Hong Kong   Set in Cloister   Book design by Teresa Kietlinski

The art was created using acrylics applied with dry brushes on multiple layers.
The painting surface was first prepared with gesso, using a sponge roller.

Grateful acknowledgment is made for permission to reprint the following copyrighted works: "Let's Count the Raindrops" from *A Nickel Buys a Rhyme* by Alan Benjamin. Copyright © 1993 by Alan Benjamin. Used by permission of HarperCollins Publishers. "The Leaves Fall Down" from *Nibble, Nibble* by Margaret Wise Brown. Copyright © 1959 by William R. Scott, Inc. Copyright renewed 1987 by Roberta Brown Rauch. Used by permission of HarperCollins Publishers. "Wouldn't You?" from *You Read to Me, I'll Read to You* by John Ciardi. Copyright © 1962 by John Ciardi. Used by permission of HarperCollins Publishers. "The Silent Snow" from *Cherry Stones! Garden Swings!* by Ivy Eastwick. Copyright © 1962, renewed 1990 by Abingdon Press. Used by permission of Abingdon Press. "June" from *Going Barefoot* by Aileen Fisher (T. Y. Crowell). Copyright © 1960 by Aileen Fisher. Copyright renewed 1988 by Aileen Fisher. Used by permission of Marian Reiner for the author. "Winter Clothes" from *The Rose on My Cake* by Karla Kuskin. Copyright © 1964, renewed 1992 by Karla Kuskin. Reprinted by permission of Scott Treimel New York.